**For the students at
Brooks Hill Elementary School —J. K.**

For my mom, Cathy, who is my hero —A. B.

A FEIWEL AND FRIENDS BOOK

An imprint of Macmillan Publishing Group, LLC • 120 Broadway, New York, NY 10271 • mackids.com

FRANKENSLIME. Text copyright © 2021 by Joy Keller. Illustrations copyright © 2021 by Ashley Belote.
All rights reserved. Printed in China by RR Donnelley Asia Printing Solutions Ltd., Dongguan City, Guangdong Province.

Our books may be purchased in bulk for promotional, educational, or business use.
Please contact your local bookseller or the Macmillan Corporate and Premium Sales Department
at (800) 221-7945 ext. 5442 or by email at MacmillanSpecialMarkets@macmillan.com.

Library of Congress Cataloging-in-Publication Data
Names: Keller, Joy, author. | Belote, Ashley, illustrator. | Title: Frankenslime / written by Joy Keller ; illustrated by Ashley Belote.
Description: First edition. | New York : Feiwel and Friends, 2021. | Audience: Ages 4-8. | Audience: Grades K-1.
Summary: Victoria and her assistant, her dog Igor, set out to make amazing slime, but one night their creation unexpectedly comes to life.
Identifiers: LCCN 2020039221 | ISBN 978-1-250-76580-2 (hardcover) | Subjects: CYAC: Scientists—Fiction. | Experiments—Fiction.
Classification: LCC PZ7.1.K4177 Fr 2021 | DDC [E]—dc23 | LC record available at https://lccn.loc.gov/2020039221

Book design by Mallory Grigg
Feiwel and Friends logo designed by Filomena Tuosto
First edition, 2021

1 3 5 7 9 10 8 6 4 2

FRANKENSLIME

Written by **Joy Keller**

Illustrated by **Ashley Belote**

Feiwel and Friends

New York

Victoria Franken was a slime scientist.

Her curiosity about slime was sparked when she stumbled upon a video of the slime-making process.

Scientific Method:
Observation
Question-?
Hypothesis
Experiment
Analysis
Conclusion

take Notes!

Inspired by her research,
Victoria scoured the house
for materials and set up a lab.
"Igor! Fetch me my tools!"

Food Coloring

Chameleons House

Don't t
pplesauc
y for a
nack!
um!

SLiMe Shininess
Matte=Not shiny
Satin=Kind of shiny
Semigloss=More shine
Gloss=Very shiny
Need sunglasses=
extremely shiny
(make with caution)

SLiMe
Diagram

Wide
Splatter

Excess
Splatter

Normal
Shine

Proper
Stretch
and Drip

Observe
SLiMe Viscosity-
the thickness of
the SLiMe

High
Viscosity

Medium
Viscosity

Low
Viscosity

CAUTION CAUTI

SLiMe
Lab
guard
Dog

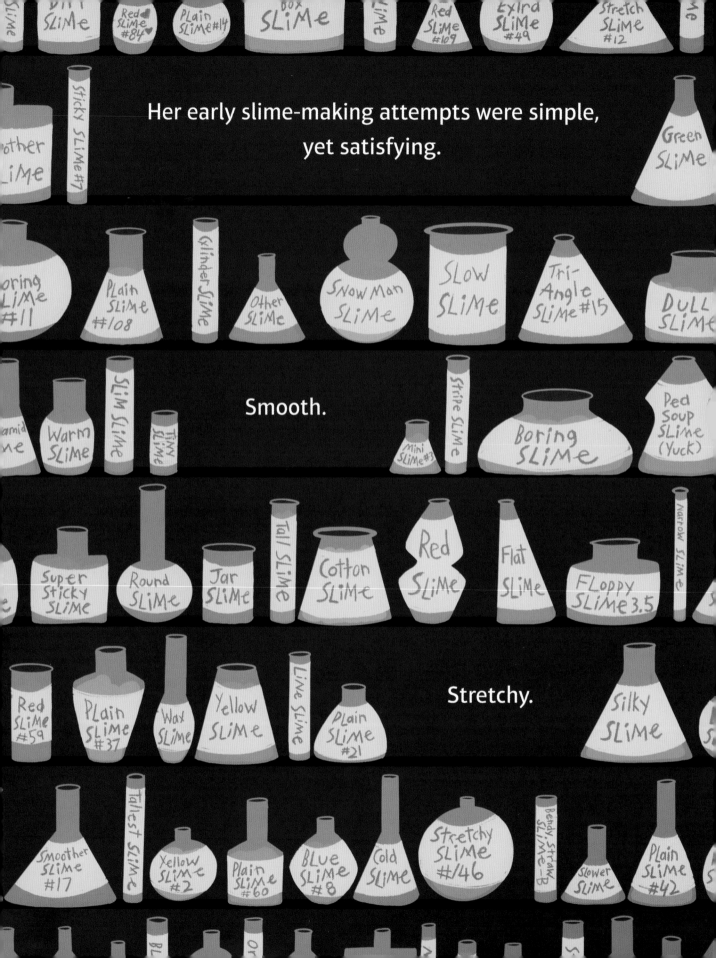

Her early slime-making attempts were simple,
yet satisfying.

Smooth.

Stretchy.

But it wasn't long before Victoria grew bored.
She daydreamed about new slimes—slimes that had
never been imagined. "Igor! We must experiment!"

Most of her slimes turned out to be . . . well, not so slimy.

This didn't deter Victoria Franken!
She took notes on every failed batch.

She changed her approach.

She tried again . . .

Poodle Puff Slime → No!

Balloon Slime → No!

and again . . .

and again . . .

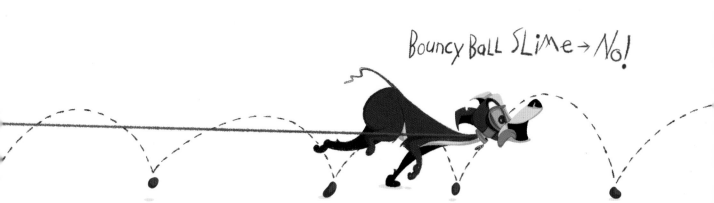

Bouncy Ball Slime → No!

. . . until she created slimes that were truly amazing.

Rainbow cloud slime.

Intergalactic space slime.

Glow-in-the-dark zombie slime.

Soon people took note of her work.
They dubbed her the Queen of Slime and lined up
to get their hands on her latest concoctions.

One night, an idea struck her. She sprang from bed and gathered her materials. "Igor! To the attic!"

While a storm raged outside,
Victoria poured and mixed
and kneaded until . . .

Victoria held her breath.
Igor whimpered.

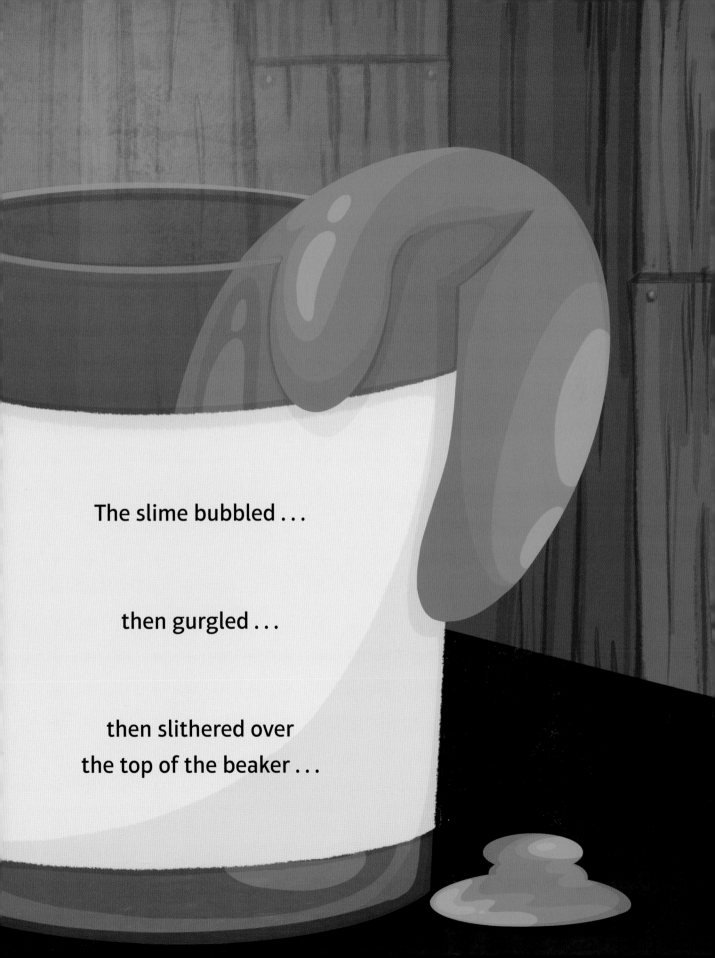

The slime bubbled . . .

then gurgled . . .

then slithered over
the top of the beaker . . .

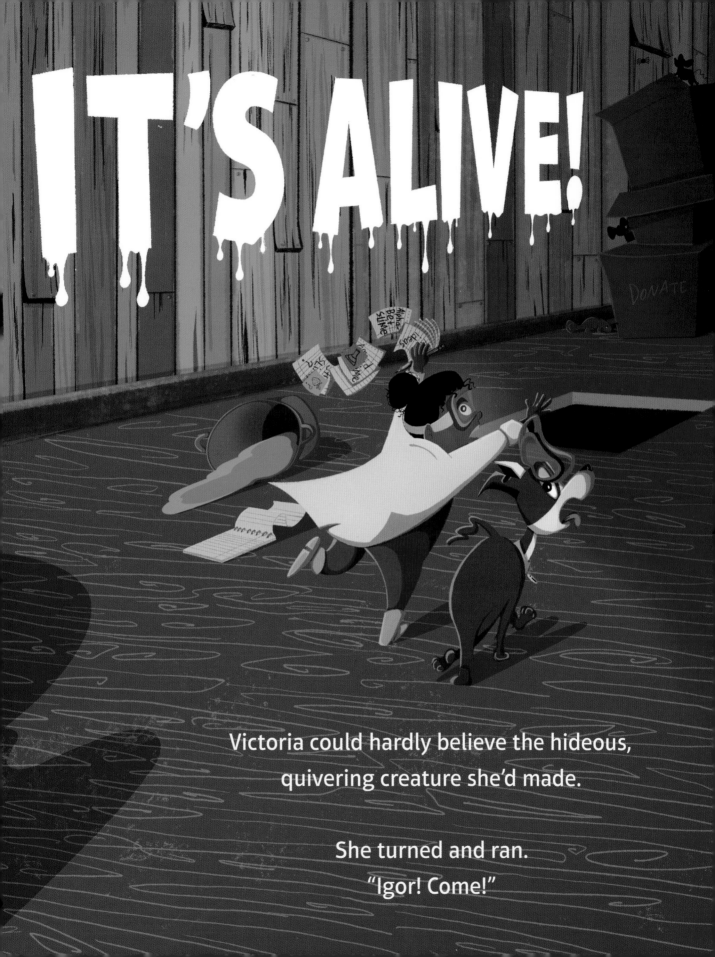

IT'S ALIVE!

Victoria could hardly believe the hideous,
quivering creature she'd made.

She turned and ran.
"Igor! Come!"

Cursing her chemistry skills,
she flew down the stairs
and slammed the attic door.

Safe from the slime on the other side,
she sank to the ground with relief . . .

. . . but not for long.

She
tried
climbing
to
safety.

"Igor! Up!"

ROPE
SLIME
For Sticky Situations

But
her
goopy
monster
defied
gravity.

On the run once more,
she took refuge under
the covers of her bed.
"Igor! Play dead!"

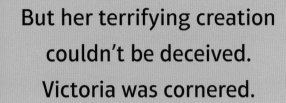

But her terrifying creation
couldn't be deceived.
Victoria was cornered.

"What do you
want from me?!"
she cried.

The slime oozed closer,
a sharp object in its sticky
clutches.

Igor growled.
Victoria cowered.

The slime reached out
and handed her . . .

How foolish of her! In all the excitement of creating the slime, Victoria had forgotten an important scientific step— recording the recipe! It was a good thing the slime had remembered.

From that day forward, Victoria had another lab partner.
Goop didn't talk much, but they made an excellent team.

"Igor! Goop!
Time to experiment!"

From the Lab of Victoria Franken

Victoria's recipe for a slime creature is top secret, but she has agreed to share some of her *other* slime recipes. You can follow her easy directions to make fun slimes of your own.

Be sure to ask an adult to be your lab assistant!

For each recipe, you'll need a medium mixing bowl, measuring cups, measuring spoons, and a mixing spoon.

Cloud Slime

Materials
1½ heaping cups foam shaving cream
food coloring of your choice
¼ cup white school glue
¼ teaspoon baking soda
1½ teaspoons saline solution

Steps

1. Put the shaving cream into a bowl. Add a few drops of food coloring and stir slowly. If you mix too quickly, the shaving cream will lose its fluffiness!

2. Add the glue and mix.

3. Add the baking soda and mix again.

4. Slowly add the saline solution, stirring as you go.

5. When the slime pulls away from the sides of the bowl and becomes hard to mix, take it out and work it with your hands. If the slime feels too sticky, rub a little saline solution on your hands to prevent the slime from sticking to your fingers. Keep going until it's the right consistency.

6. Play with your super-fluffy cloud slime!

Tip: If you want to make Victoria's *rainbow* cloud slime, make several batches of cloud slime in different colors and swirl them together!

Osage City Public Library
515 Main Street
Osage City, Kansas 66523
www.osagecitylibrary.org

Intergalactic Space Slime

Materials
½ cup clear school glue
½ cup water
black acrylic paint
1 teaspoon silver or black glitter
⅓ cup liquid starch

Steps

1. Mix the glue and water together in a bowl.

2. Add enough black paint to make the glue mixture as dark as space, then add the glitter. Mix well.

3. Slowly add the starch, stirring constantly as you go. Keep stirring until the slime starts to pull away from the sides of the bowl.

4. Leave the slime in the bowl for about two minutes, then take it out and work it in your hands until it's the right consistency.

5. Play with your intergalactic space slime!

Tip: To make your slime look even more stellar, mix up extra batches of slime made with blue and red paint. Then swirl them into your black slime for the ultimate intergalactic effect!

Glow-in-the-Dark Zombie Slime

Materials
¾ cup clear school glue (or 6 oz)
½ teaspoon baking soda
¼ cup water
1 tablespoon glow-in-the-dark paint
green food coloring
1 tablespoon saline solution

Steps

1. Mix the glue, baking soda, water, paint, and a few drops of food coloring together in a bowl.

2. Slowly add the saline solution, stirring as you go.

3. Rub a little saline solution on your hands to prevent the slime from sticking to your fingers, then work the slime in your hands. It will be extra sticky and disgusting at first (after all, it's zombie slime). Keep going until it's the right consistency.

4. Play with your ooey-gooey zombie slime!

Tip: For extra fun, mix in gross zombie parts, such as googly eyes, plastic fingers, etc. Get creative!

Note: Slime results may vary, depending on the brand of ingredients you use. If you aren't using the *same* exact ingredients as Victoria, you may need to do a little experimenting yourself! Here are helpful hints for a smooth slime-making experience:

- If your slime is too sticky, try adding a little more saline solution or starch.
- If your slime is too rubbery or breaks easily, try softening it with a little lotion or warm water.
- Always remember to wash your hands after playing with your slime!

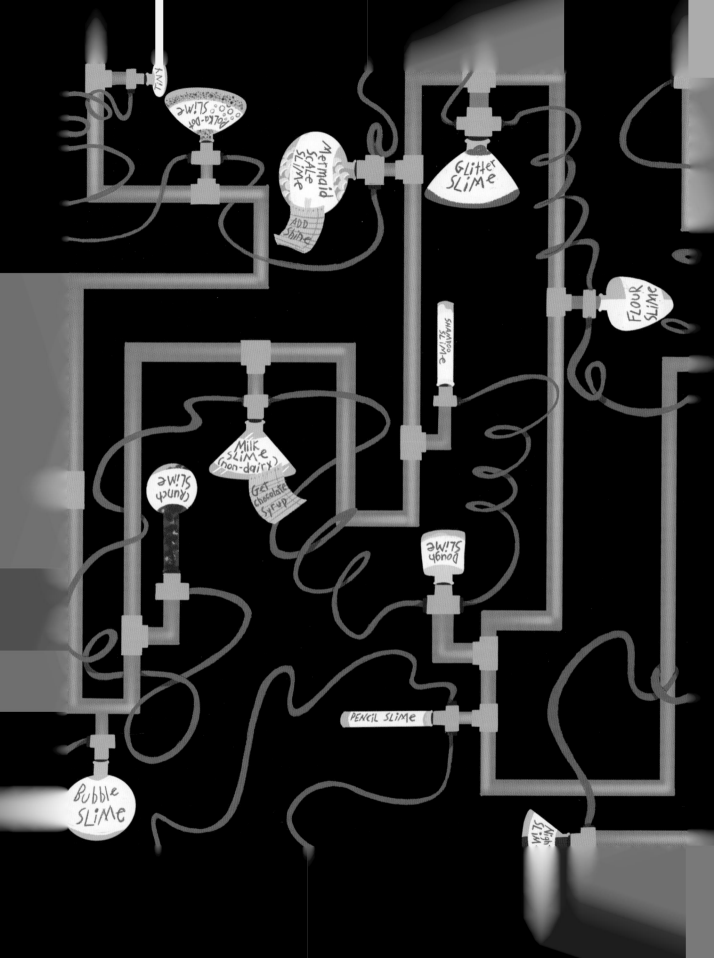